a minedition book

published by Penguin Young Readers Group

Illustrations copyright © 2005 by Lisbeth Zwerger
Rights arranged with "minedition" Rights and Licensing AG, Zurich, Switzerland.
Coproduction with Michael Neugebauer Publishing Ltd. Hong Kong.
All rights reserved. This book, or parts thereof, may not be reproduced in any form without
permission in writing from the publisher, Penguin Young Readers Group, 345 Hudson Street,
New York, NY 10014.

Published simultaneously in Canada.
Manufactured in Hong Kong by Wide World Ltd.
Typesetting in Neugebauer Rustica and Neugebauer Kursiv designed by
Friedrich Neugebauer; digitised by Jovica Veljovic.
Color separation by Fotoreproduzioni Grafiche, Verona, Italy.

Library of Congress Cataloging-in-Publication Data available upon request.

ISBN 0-698-40030-5
10 9 8 7 6 5 4 3 2 1
First Impression

For more information please visit our website: www.minedition.com

THE NIGHT BEFORE CHRISTMAS

BY CLEMENT CLARKE MOORE
WITH PICTURES BY LISBETH ZWERGER

MINEDITION

'Twas the night before Christmas, when all through the house

Not a creature was stirring, not even a mouse;

The stockings were hung by the chimney with care,

In hopes that Saint Nicholas soon would be there.

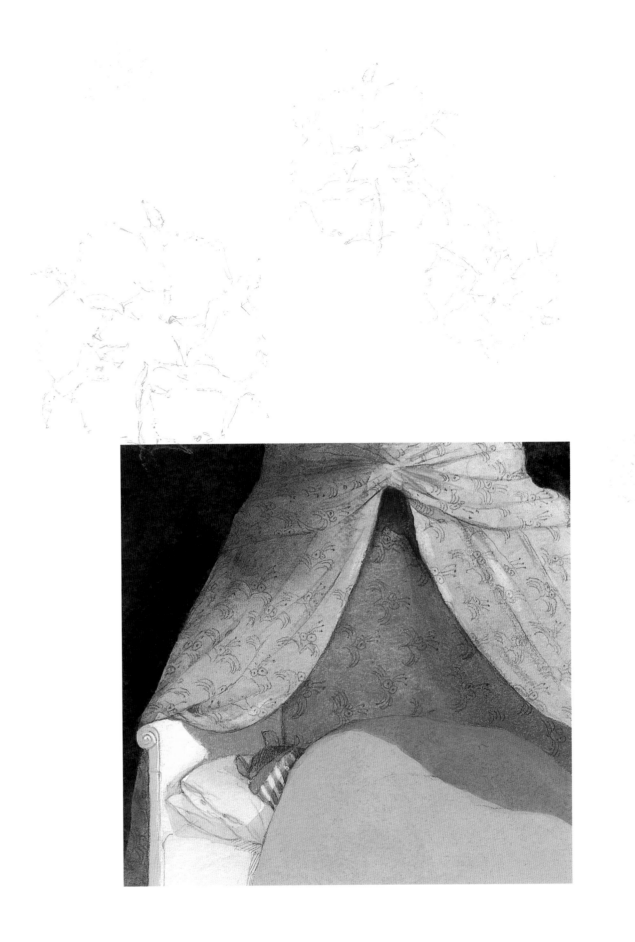

The children were nestled all snug in their beds,

While visions of sugar-plums danced in their heads;

And Mamma in her kerchief, and I in my cap,

Had just settled down for a long winter's nap,

When out on the lawn there rose such a clatter,

I sprang from the bed to see what was the matter.

Away to the window I flew like a flash,

Tore open the shutters and threw up the sash.

The moon on the breast of the new-fallen snow

Gave a luster of mid-day to objects below,

When, what to my wondering eyes should appear,

But a miniature sleigh, and eight tiny reindeer,

With a little old driver, so lively and quick,

I knew in a moment it must be St. Nick.

More rapid than eagles his coursers they came,

And he whistled, and shouted, and called them by name —

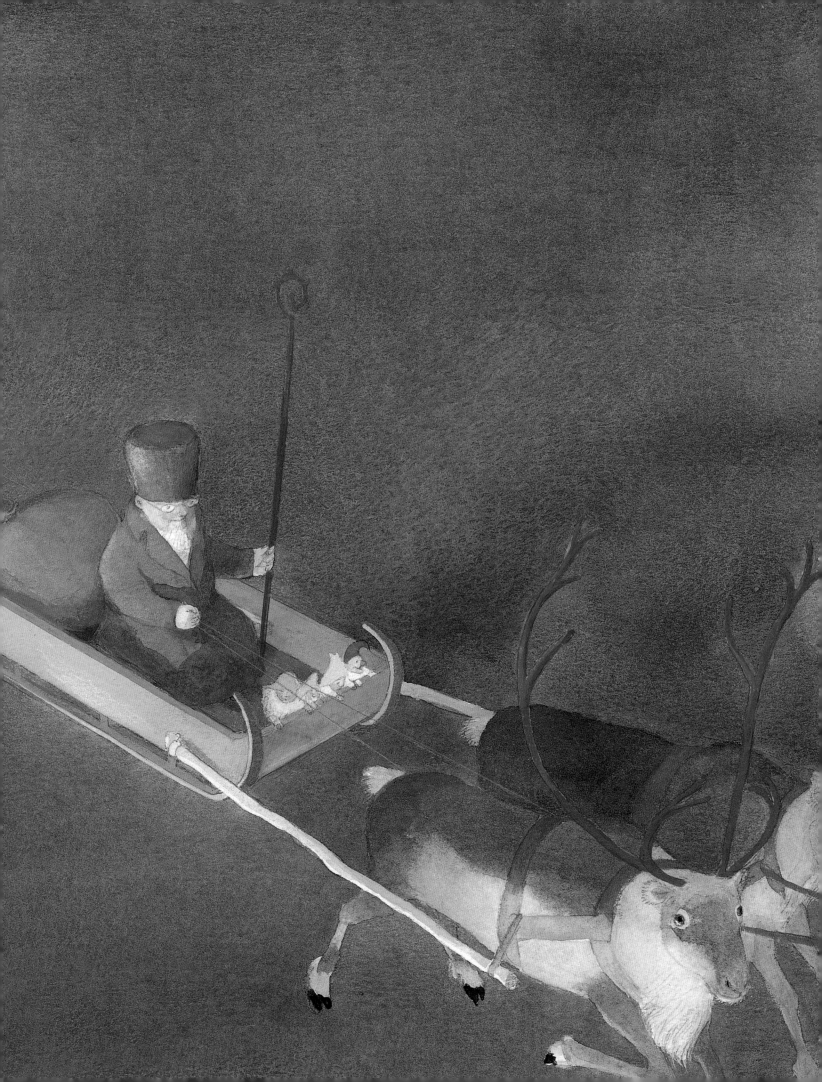

"Now, Dasher, now, Dancer! Now, Prancer and Vixen!

On, Comet! On, Cupid! On, Donder and Blitzen!

To the top of the porch, to the top of the wall,

Now, dash away, dash away, dash away all!"

As dry leaves that before the wild hurricane fly,

When they meet with an obstacle, mount to the sky,

So up to the house-top the coursers they flew,

With the sleigh full of toys, — and St. Nicholas too.

And then in a twinkling, I heard on the roof

The prancing and pawing of each little hoof.

As I drew in my head, and was turning around,

Down the chimney St. Nicholas came with a bound.

He was dressed all in fur, from his head to his foot,

And his clothes were all tarnished with ashes and soot;

A bundle of toys he had flung on his back,

And he looked like a peddler just opening his pack.

His eyes – how they twinkled! His dimples how merry!

His cheeks were like roses, his nose like a cherry!

His droll little mouth was drawn up like a bow,

And the beard on his chin was as white as the snow.

The stump of the pipe he held tight in his teeth,

And the smoke, it encircled his head like a wreath.

He had a broad face and a little round belly,

That shook when he laughed like a bowlful of jelly.

He was chubby and plump, a right jolly old elf,

And I laughed when I saw him, in spite of myself.

A wink of his eye and a twist of his head,

Soon gave me to know I had nothing to dread.

He spoke not a word, but went straight to his work,

And filled all the stockings, then turned with a jerk,

And laying his finger aside of his nose,

And giving a nod, up the chimney he rose.

He sprang to his sleigh, to his team gave a whistle,

And away they all flew like the down of a thistle.

But I heard him exclaim, ere he drove out of sight,

"Merry Christmas to All,

and to All a Good Night."